Hello.
Who can help me find
my special shape?

Goz goes to see his friend
in the stable.

Neigh!

Goz goes to see his friends
by the wall.

Scratch
Scratch

Goz goes to see his friends in the roof.

Flip
Flap

Goz goes to see his friend on her nest.

Cluck cluck

Goz hears splashing
from the pond.

Splash
Splish

The circle is my special shape too. . .
and round . . . .